WILDCATS

If found please
return this book to
TROY BOLTON
East High School
Albuquerque,
New Mexico

Scholastic Inc.

New York · Toronto · London · Auckland · Sydney
Mexico City · New Delhi · Hong Kong · Buenos Aires

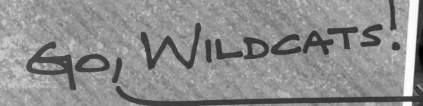

Go, Wildcats!

FROM THE DESK OF COACH BOLTON

Dear Troy:

I am very pleased to inform you that your performance at tryouts has secured you a place on East High's Wildcats Basketball Team.

Being a member of the Wildcats is a very serious commitment. You will be required to practice every day after school as well as attend and play in all games. Games may be at home or you may have to travel with the team to play at other high schools. Should the team make it to the championships, the game location may also require travel.

If you are injured, you are still required to come to practice and learn what you can from the sidelines. Missing practice or games due to illness must be followed up with a doctor's note. Lateness to practice will not be tolerated.

Being a member of the Wildcats team is the experience of a lifetime! You will have to work hard, but you will have fun doing it. A team is only as strong as its teammates.

Welcome to the team!

Sincerely,

COACH BOLTON

Coach Bolton

EAST HIGH SCHOOL
300 S. Wildcat Avenue · Albuquerque, NM

CONGRATS, SON! I'M SO PROUD OF YOU!

WILD

WILDCATS
ATH DEPT
BASKETBALL
Association Handbook

Team Roster

Troy Bolton	14	Captain/Forward
Chad Danforth	8	Guard
Jason Cross	23	Forward
Zeke Baylor	32	Center
Austin Anderson		Guard
Adam		...ard
		...ward
		...rd
		...rd
M...		...rward
Be...		...ward

NEW LINEUP!

Troy—

Here's the new line-up
for this season.
Congratulations!

Dad

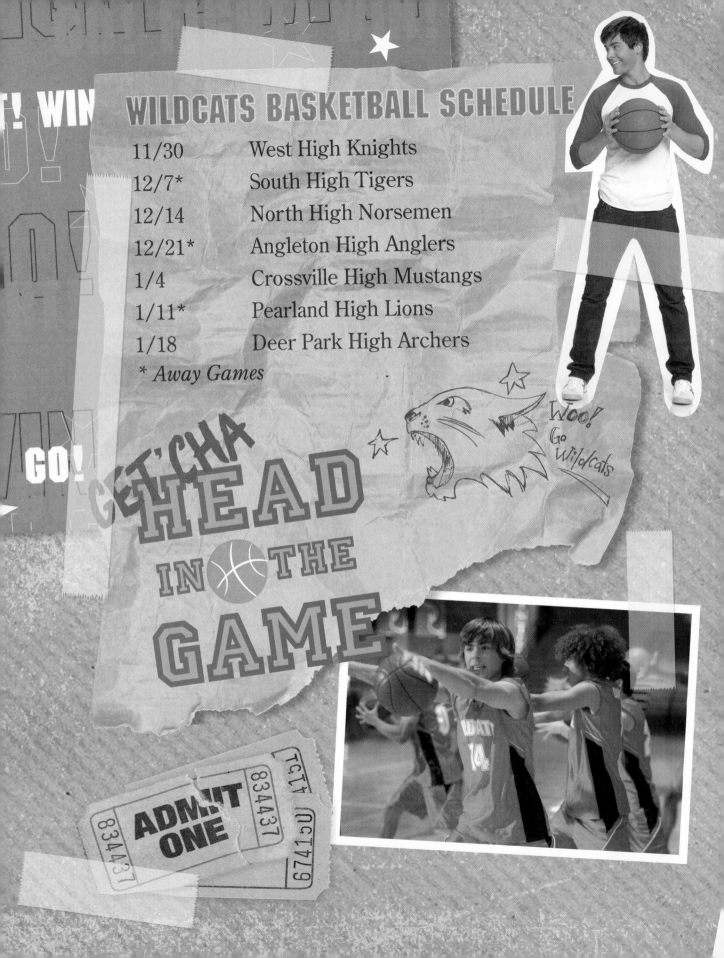

WILDCATS BASKETBALL SCHEDULE

11/30	West High Knights
12/7*	South High Tigers
12/14	North High Norsemen
12/21*	Angleton High Anglers
1/4	Crossville High Mustangs
1/11*	Pearland High Lions
1/18	Deer Park High Archers

* *Away Games*

GET'CHA HEAD IN THE GAME

Woo! Go Wildcats

WIN! GO!

ADMIT ONE 834437 834437 0741790

Dear Wildcats,

This is it, team! It's been an amazing year, and we have one more game to go. As you know, this isn't just any game but the championship. It's time to topple West High—and we are the team to do it! You all have worked so hard this season. I'm proud of each and every one of you. No matter how the score comes out, you're all winners.

Proud to be your coach,
Coach Bolton

Ms. Darbus

Dear Sports People:
It has come to my attention that Coach Bolton's practices and my latest and greatest musical's rehearsals have been scheduled for the same time. While I am quite surprised that this is an issue at all please be assured that I will take the matter up with Coach Bolton immediately so that you can kick your field goals or practice tackling or whatever it is you people do in the gym.

Sincerely,
Ms. Darbus

FROM THE DESK OF PRINCIPAL MATSUI

Congratulations on winning the championship against the West High Knights. You have made me—and all the students and faculty at this school—very proud. Go, Wildcats!

Principal Matsui

GAME ON!

TEAM PRACTICES
Mon, Tues, Wed, Thurs

3:30 sharp
No exceptions!

14

Team:	Jersey Color		Record		Coach
East High	Red	Conference: 2	Overall: 6-2		J. Bolton
Date: November 3	At: Home		Referee: M. Monitello		

Pos.	Player Name	Quarters Played	Personal Fouls	Player Number	2's	3's		F	Total Pt
F	Troy Bolton		1 2 (3) 4 5	14	⊘				
F	Jason Cross		1 (2) 3 4 5	23	1			1	
C	Zeke Baylor		1 2 3 (4) 5	32	⊘				2
G	Chad Danforth		1 2 (3) 4 5	8	1			⊘	2
G	Austin Anderson		1 (2) 3 4 5	11	4			3	11
F		5		1⊘	2			⊘	4
								2	2

"If you play basketball, you'll end up on the cereal box."
—Chad

"You're the playmaker."
—Troy

"The team voted you the game ball."
—Chad

"Get'cha head in the game!"
—Troy

"What team? Wildcats!"
—Chad

WILDCATS

Get'cha HEAD in the

WILDCATS RULES

→ AND Troy Bolton's

1. Constant practice breeds perfection.
   Dream big.

2. Keep your eye on the prize.
   Make it happen!

3. Come prepared.
   Limit TV during the week. Manage your time better.

4. Be respectful of your coaches and teammates.
   Practice, practice, practice!

5. Follow the plan.
   Structure time better.

6. Work hard, play hard.
   Eat healthy.

7. Be on time.
   Get'cha head in the game – and keep it there!

8. Keep your focus.
   Do Drills!!

9. Work as a team.
   Never let them see your fear.

10. Play your best, no matter what.
    Keep up your grades.

11. Have fun!
    —— YES!!!!!

EA

THE TEAM IS YOU. YOU ARE THE TEAM!
—COACH B

YOU GOT GAME?

Coach

Troy really
gets his head
in the game!

You're the playmaker!

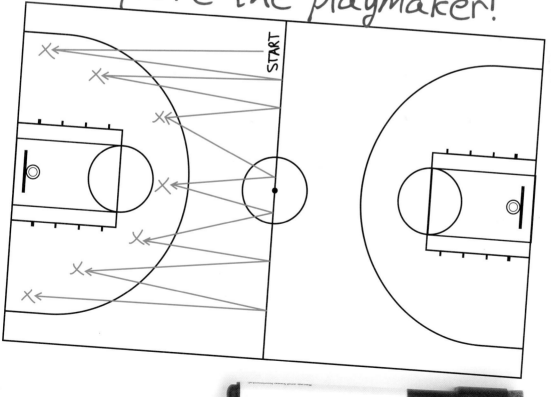

START

WILDCATS

Get to know your

TROY BOLTON #14

Favorite food: Cheeseburger

Favorite color: Red

Favorite way to chill out: Shooting hoops in the backyard

Favorite quote: "Sports do not build character. They reveal it." —John Wooden

Favorite book: To Kill a Mockingbird by Harper Lee

Activities: Varsity basketball (captain), golf team, winter musical

ZEKE BAYLOR #32

Favorite food: Pastries

Favorite color: Gold

Favorite way to chill out: Listening to music

Favorite quote: "Part of the secret of success in life is to eat what you like and let the food fight it out inside." —Mark Twain

Favorite book: The Joy of Cooking

Activities: Varsity basketball, Young Bakers of America

SPOTLIGHT

favorite basketball team!

CHAD DANFORTH #8

Favorite food: French fries

Favorite color: Green

Favorite way to chill out: Watching standup comedy on TV

Favorite quote: "Basketball is like photography, if you don't focus, all you have is the negative." —Dan Frisby

Favorite book: Any joke collection

Activities: Varsity basketball, track and field

JASON CROSS #23

Favorite food: Enchiladas

Favorite color: Black

Favorite way to chill out: Practicing tai chi

Favorite quote: "It ain't over 'til it's over." —Yogi Berra

Favorite book: The Hobbit by J.R.R. Tolkein

Activities: Varsity basketball

EAST HIGH

EHS

PEP
RALLY

Our cheerleaders do a great job!

Wildcats Cheer

Come on, Wildcats! Who are fans?
Let us see you clap your hands!
Come on, Wildcats!
Get the beat!
Let us hear you stomp your feet!
Come on, Wildcats!
Get the groove!
Let us see you jump and move!
Go, Wildcats! (clap)
Go, Wildcats! (stomp)
Yay!!!

WildCATS in the news

SPORTS

February 28

WILDCATS GAINING GROUND

By Charlie Holt
After a rocky beginning, plagued by missteps and injuries, the East High Wildcats are finally getting in their groove. Captain Troy Bolton led his team

to victory against the Angleton High Anglers. It was a close game that even went into overtime. But the Wildcats came through, winning 56-54.

Fresh off their win, the Wildcats defeated both Crossville and Pearland High. The success at North High was especially hard for the Norsemen since they had home court advantage. But it wasn't enough to stop the Wildcats from clobbering them 60-47.

Could East High be heading toward the championship? Only time will tell!

WILDCAT Troy Bolton leads East to a victory over Angleton High.

WILDCATS CENTER TAKES THE CAKE

By Peter Wright

Zeke Baylor is adding a new set of skills to his long list of basketball tricks. The Wildcats center is baking up a storm and loving it, and is now an official member of the Young Bakers of America.

Zeke's friends and teammates have nothing but rave reviews for the new chef. "Zeke's cookies are amazing," says team captain Troy Bolton. "I've never had better."

Just like his three-point shot is the highlight of his basketball game, Zeke's crème brulee is the highlight of his cooking. He's been getting all kinds of requests to make desserts for school banquets and special events.

Who knows? This star player's future may lie in the kitchen and not on the court.

YOU ARE SOOOO DRAMATIC...STICK WITH THE THEATER.

THE POINT IS TO WIN THE GAME!

It's not ridiculous, it's fun!

WHY B-BALL?

By Sharpay Evans

People! What is the fascination with basketball? I mean, you sweat. You wear those hideous uniforms. And you just run back and forth...and back and forth...while a clock runs down. Can someone please tell me the point??

On the other hand, the drama club works hard to develop an engaging story and uplifting music to fill the auditorium with laughter and joy. I wish this school would stop focusing so much on the ridiculous game of basketball. After all, when there is greatness among you (like myself) that should be recognized.

WE ARE THE CHAMPIONS!

By Charlie Holt

In a nail-biting championship game, the East High Wildcats emerged victorious over their longtime rival, the West High Knights, with a final score of 68-67.

The Wildcats and the Knights were well matched and neck in neck from the beginning. At the end of the first period the score was tied 8 to 8.

Then a funny thing happened on the way to the championship…there was a power surge. The lights and scoreboard flashed and the game was halted. For public safety, everyone was quickly ushered out of the gym.

Less than an hour later, the power in the gym was restored and the

WILDCAT Troy Bolton leads East High to a championship victory.

Thanks, guys!

game continued. No one knows exactly what happened, but Principal Matsui has said he will look into it.

Wildcat spirit was definitely in the house during halftime as the cheerleaders performed. Fans were on their feet and you could feel the excitement buzzing in the air. A lot was riding on this game. East High had lost the championship to West High three years in a row. Going into the second half, it seemed very clear that both teams were focused and determined to win.

During the second half, the Wildcats came out fighting, but so did the Knights. The score was tied with five minutes left on the clock. With 11 seconds to go, Troy Bolton raced the ball down the court, passed to teammate Zeke Baylor who passed right back to Bolton. Bolton shot a two-pointer

right at the buzzer, winning the championship game for the East High Wildcats. The crowd erupted and the Wildcats celebrated their new and well-earned championship title.

Our fans ROCK! The support was great.

Gabriella is the best. Together 4-Ever

Good Luck, Troy! GO, WILDCATS!!! —Gabriella

Q&A WITH TROY BOLTON

by Chad Danforth

Let's get to know MVP Troy Bolton both on and off the court.

Chad Danforth: Looking back at the season, could you have predicted you'd end up as MVP?

Troy Bolton: It's hard to predict. I think the team worked really hard all year, and despite some bumps along the road, we all pulled together and did our best.

CD: You were the first sophomore ever to make starting varsity. Did you feel a lot of pressure?

TB: Sometimes. It's easy to get caught up in that, but I find if I just focus on the game and being a member of the team, everything's cool.

CD: How do you prepare for a game?

TB: Prepare? What do you mean? I just show up and the magic happens. [Laughs.] No, seriously, though, we do a lot of prep before a game.

CD: More than just showing up to practice?

TB: Yeah, man. Right before the game starts, I really do my best to focus and concentrate on what needs to happen to win that game. I try to block everything else out.

CD: Does it work?

TB: Most of the time. Except when you harass me before a game.

CD: Hey, man. That's how I prep for a game!

TB: [Laughs.] I think we have to find something new for you to do.

CD: Do you think you have it harder than the rest of us because your father is the coach?

TB: We're all in this together! But I think ultimately, my dad and I want the same thing: the best for the team. Being a former basketball player himself, I can't blame him for wanting me to succeed.

CD: What other sports do you like to play?

TB: Golf.

CD: Do you find it hard to juggle schoolwork and all the extracurricular activities?

TB: Sure. But you're only here once (hopefully!), so why not take advantage of all the school has to offer? Besides, if you can do those activities with your friends, then it's even more fun.

CD: College or NBA?

TB: College. Definitely.

CD: Chocolate or vanilla?

TB: What does that have to do with anything?

CD: Nothing, but I wanted to keep this interesting.

TB: Isn't it a little late for that?

CD: Funny, Bolton, funny. So where do you see yourself in 10 years?

TB: Older.

CD: Touché.

TB: Hopefully playing basketball, hanging out with my friends, and of course, spending time with Gabriella. And hopefully, we'll be done with this interview by then!

Woo!
Go
Wildcats

FROM THE DESK OF
COACH BOLTON

PEP TALK NOTES

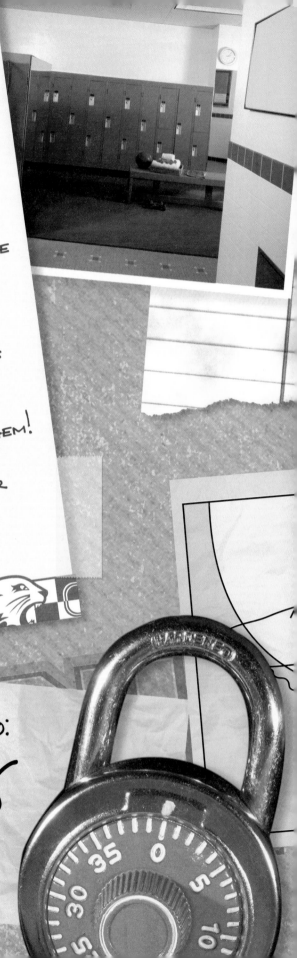

* The North High Norsemen have beaten us too many times. It's time to make our stand. Today is the day! You've been working hard for months. Let me see what you've got out there.

* Remember—this team does not exist unless each and every one of you is focused on our goal.

* Now let's go out there and get them!

* What team? Wildcats! Get your head in the game!

WILD CATS

Locker Combo:

14-22-46

TOP SECRET

East High Wildcats Fight Song

Yay, Wildcats! Scratch and claw
Your way to victory with tooth and paw!
Fight! Fight! With all your might!
So we may cheer our team tonight!
Go, Wildcats! Go, Wildcats! Go, Wildcats!
GROWWWL!!!

HISTORY REPEATS ITSELF

By Charlie Holt

The Bolton family will surely be celebrating for quite some time. Following in his father's footsteps, sophmore Troy Bolton was named MVP after leading his team to a whopping victory against their long-time rival, the West High Knights. It was a close game, with the final score coming in at 68-67.

"Not only is there an element of tradition in winning this," Bolton said, "but there is a great sense of pride in being able to share this experience with my father."

When I reminded Coach Bolton that he said, "This is the greatest day of my life," upon his winning in 1981, the coach felt an update was due. "Today is the greatest day of my life. Seeing Troy win is better than winning myself."

This is the first time that a father and son have been awarded the MVP, but with Bolton playing again next year, history just might repeat itself.

2/13

EAST HIGH WILDCATS MOST VALUABLE PLAYER

"SPIDER" BILL NATRINE	1972
JACK BOLTON	1981
"THE THUNDERCLAP" HAP HADDON	1995
SAM NEDLER "SAMMY SLAMMER JAMMER"	2002
TROY BOLTON	2008

Gotta keep my grades up!

TROY—

JUST A REMINDER THAT THERE WILL BE COLLEGE SCOUTS AT TONIGHT'S GAME! NO PRESSURE, BUT GET OUT THERE AND SHOW THEM YOUR BEST!

LOVE,

DAD

I can't wait to play at a place like this!

University of Albuquerque

Dear Troy:

I'm writing to tell you about the wonderful athletic program at the University of Albuquerque. Our athletes have a long tradition of athletic and academic excellence. Our students go on to successful athletic and professional careers in a wide variety of fields.

The University of Albuquerque also offers top-of-the-line facilities, including our brand-new basketball arena. We also have a nationally-recognized chemistry laboratory, a state-of-the-art observatory, and high-tech lecture halls—not to mention cozy dorms and a top-notch cafeteria!

We had the pleasure of watching you play in this season's championship game and were very impressed with what we saw. We look forward to following your future games and hope you'll keep the University of Albuquerque in mind when you apply to college.

Sincerely,

Mac Johnson
Head Basketball Coach
University of Albuquerque

GO, REDHAWKS!

Honoring Wiley the Wildcat

It's no mystery who keeps the Wildcats spirit alive throughout the year and really gets the crowd going during games. Wiley the Wildcat, East High's one and only mascot, who proudly wears the number 1 on his chest, is truly the heart and soul of East High. And, as Ms. Darbus knows, he's quite a good dancer, too.

We've all seen Wiley's high energy flips and jumps pump up a discouraged crowd. In fact, it's safe to say that our championship team owes a lot of its success to Wiley.

Despite all of his amazing contributions, a mascot doesn't always get the thanks and attention he deserves. So, Wildcats, next time you're at a game, make sure you take the time to notice one of the less celebrated members of the team, and give an extra cheer for him.

Wiley the Wildcat in action, pumping up the crowd.

You've heard about us
Remember our name
The Wildcats are here
To win this game!
Catch the spirit
That we create
'Cause tonight's the night
We dominate!

Let's go, boys,
Shoot for two
C'mon, Wildcats
Put it through!
You might be good at football
You might be good at track
But when it comes to
basketball,
You might as well
step back!

Dribble it.
Pass it.
We want a basket!
Go! Fight! Win!
Sink it in!
To the hoop!

To the hoop!
Now shoot, Wildcats, shoot!

Wildcats, let's shake it.
Victory, let's take it!
Move the ball
Down the floor
Score! Score! Score!

Hey, Wildcats
Set the pace
Hey, Wildcats
Rock this place!
Genie, genie,
Grant my wish
Let me hear that ball
Go swish!

Defense attack!
Get that ball back!
Got that ball
So what do you do?
Shoot two and put it through!

 # WILDCATS

wow!

Team spirit

Hangin' with Gabriella

Chad & Taylor lookin' fine

Troy sings his heart out.

GOOF AROUND

The winning team

Let's celebrate!

I can't get up.

Off the court and onstage!

END OF SEASON BANQUET

ZEKE'S CRÈME BRULEE WAS AWESOME!

WILDCATS

Welcome to the East High End of Season Banquet!

This is our way of thanking you for another great season. Go, Wildcats!

Thanks to the parents who brought food—and a special thanks to our own Zeke Baylor for the fantastic desserts.

Enjoy the food and fun! You deserve it.

Sincerely,
Your coaches

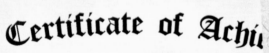

Certificate of Achi

presented to

Troy Bolton

Most Valuable Playe

for outstanding merit

COACH BOLTON

GRANTED BY

Principal Matsui

GRANTED BY

Got my varsity letter!

Dear players,

Thank you for another fantastic season. You guys put your all into the team, and boy did it pay off. I hope you're all very proud of yourselves and your places on this championship team! I'm very happy for you and your accomplishments, and am proud to call myself your coach.

Enjoy your summer, stay in shape, and I look forward to seeing you next year for another great season.

Sincerely,

Coach Bolton

Can't wait for next season!

Based on the Disney Channel Original Movie
"High School Musical," written by Peter Barsocchini.

Based on the Disney Channel Original Movie
"High School Musical 2," written by Peter Barsocchini.

Based on Characters Created by Peter Barsocchini.
Copyright © 2008 Disney Enterprises, Inc. All rights reserved.
Published by Scholastic Inc. SCHOLASTIC and associated logos are trademarks
and/or registered trademarks of Scholastic Inc.

Printed in the U.S.A.

First Scholastic printing, January 2009

12 11 10 9 8 7 6 5 4 3 2 1   8 9 10 11 12 13/0

ISBN-13: 978-0-545-10720-4

ISBN-10: 0-545-10720-2

Text by Annie Auerbach and Robin Lyon
Design by Aruna Goldstein